ALL FOR YOU BUBBA

A modern family story of separation, divorce, and co-parenting.

By Jimmy Lee
(Dedicated to my daughter)

Copyright © 2024 Jimmy Lee

All Rights Reserved

No part of this book is to be reproduced, transmitted in any form or means; electronic or mechanical, stored in a retrieval system, photocopied, recorded, scanned, or otherwise. Any of these actions require the proper written permission of the author.

Acknowledgements:

I would like to first and foremost recognize my daughter Avery "Bubba" Lee for inspiring this book. The wonderful illustrations have been done by the super talented Ernie Francis. Avery's mom has also played a key part in making this transition as amicable as possible in an effort to have our daughter's well being as the #1 priority. Finally, I would like to thank my parents, sisters, and friends for all of the support during this process.

Author

This is my first book and never imagined publishing something in my life. But writing this book and collaborating with Ernie has been a wonderful therapeutic experience during such a difficult transition.

FOREWARD

This book was not motivated for monetary reasons.
Firstly, the impetus behind this initiative was to try and
navigate through the crazy maze that is
separation and divorce.
I can only hope that this book will help our daughter
(and other kids) understand this difficult process.
Secondly, we hope you can receive significant
value from this book.
For parents, you are not alone!

This book is a personal one that reflects our
family situation, so I do realize that many separated/divorced
situations are not as amicable.
My intent was never to have this as a one size fits all,
but rather sharing my story and what I learned.

All for you Bubba, is why we will always be
a family even though Mommy and Daddy will live apart
from each other.
Don't let anyone ever tell you what a family
should look like.

All for you Bubba, we haven't told you what was happening because we needed grown up help on what to say to you. But we know you are smart enough to realize something was going on.

All for you Bubba, is why Mommy and Daddy cry sometimes out of the blue because this is hard for both of us but we will get through it.

All for you Bubba, Mommy and Daddy are doing what is best for us, and trying to be better people, so we can always be at our best for you.

Bubba, I know you will wish
that Mommy and Daddy will get back together.
But we couldn't fix everything and never showed you what
a loving marriage looks like. We wish we were like the
Disney prince and princess dolls that you play with.

All for you Bubba, we want you to know it was
never your fault that Mommy and Daddy
will live apart from each other,
not even 2% like the milk
you like to have with your yummy snacks.

All for you Bubba, we know you will be BIG MAD over this.
We understand…
So we will always be here to talk, hug, or just give
you the space you need.

All for you Bubba we will make a schedule that works
so you have daddy time,
mommy time,
and also family time together.

All for you Bubba, we both want to be there for your most important moments in life. The 1st day of kindergarten, your 5th birthday, and whenever you need us most.

All for you Bubba, I will put my phone away when it's daddy-daughter time and give you 100% of my attention. Unless when we are taking funny pictures together.

All for you Bubba, we will never stop having family huggles especially when you need us the most.

All for you Bubba, Daddy will never play it too cool
with you. I will pick up on the first ring
when you call and I will respond right away
when you message me.

All for you Bubba, Daddy will be moving out to a place nearby, so I will be nice and close to you. Remember you said you were kind of jelly that your best friend was moving to a condo, now you can come visit daddy anytime.

All for you Bubba, daddy will sometimes stay for bedtime so you will have the sweetest candy dreams.

All for you Bubba, in this time of darkness,
you have been our moonlight off the ocean.

All for you Bubba, Daddy wrote this book to help our family and other little boys or girls going through the same thing (you are not alone). We love you so much and that will never change.

Meet our daughter Bubba

Age: Not a baby anymore, she's a big girl now
Interest: Disney and LOL dolls
Best friend: Too many to count
Favourite Princess: Tie between Ariel and Elsa
Favourite food: Tie between Korean bbq and Pizza
Best words to describe her: Bold, sassy, and smart

Other important facts:
- Night owl even without naps
- Must have juju when she sleeps, will have to wake up in the middle of night to find juju if it's missing
- Doesn't wear pyjamas when sleeping, loves running around au naturel
- Demands I bring her at least 3 snacks when I pick her up from school

---

For questions/inquiries/updates please visit:
@all4ububba all4ububba@gmail.com

On Deck: "All for you Jimmy" book coming soon!
(or might be out by the time you read this)

Special thank you's: Avery Lee, Sarah Chung, my parents & sisters, Ernie Francis, Kris B, Othership crew, Warehouse Yonge/Dundas

Manufactured by Amazon.ca
Bolton, ON